Goodwin

MW01010589

STEGOSAURUS
(steg-o-SAW-rus)

SPINOSAURUS
(SPY-no-SAW-rus)

DIPLODOCUS
(di-PLOD-o-cuss)

TRICERATOPS
(try-SARE-ah-tops)

COMPSOGNATHUS
(komp-sog-NAY-thuss)

For Ben, Adam and Jack

First edition for the United States and Canada published 1992 by Barron's
Educational Series, Inc.

First published in Great Britain 1992 by Simon & Schuster Young Books,
Wolsey House, Wolsey Road, Hemel Hempstead, Herts., HP2 4SS.

Text copyright © M. Christina Butler 1992
Illustrations copyright © Val Biro 1992

All rights reserved.
No part of this book may be reproduced in any form, by photostat,
microfilm, xerography, or any other means, or incorporated into
any information retrieval system, electronic or mechanical,
without the written permission of the copyright owner.

All inquiries should be addressed to:
Barron's Educational Series, Inc.
250 Wireless Boulevard
Hauppauge, New York 11788

Library of Congress Catalog Card No. 92-4134

International Standard Book No. 0-8120-6297-3 (hardcover)
International Standard Book No. 0-8120-1379-4 (pbk)

Library of Congress Cataloging-in-Publication Data
Butler, M. Christina.
    The dinosaur egg mystery / M. Christina Butler: illustrated by
Val Biro.
        p.   cm.
    Summary: Different dinosaurs claim a big white egg as their own
until it hatches and they find out what was inside it.
    ISBN 0-8120-6297-3.—ISBN 0-8120-1379-4 (pbk.)
    [1. Dinosaurs—Fiction.] I. Biro, Val, 1921– ill. II. Title.
PZ7.B97738Di   1992
[E]—dc20   92-4134
                                           CIP
                                           AC

PRINTED IN BELGIUM
2345   987654321

The Dinosaur Egg Mystery

M. Christina Butler

ILLUSTRATED BY
VAL BIRO

BARRON'S

A long time ago when the dinosaurs lived ...

a big white egg lay in the sand.

A sea serpent saw the egg in the sand and wanted it for lunch.

"Don't you dare touch my egg," cried an angry Diplodocus. "That egg belongs to me."

When the sea serpent had gone, Diplodocus rolled the egg away from the sea and into the forest.

"I'll hide it under those leaves," she said. "No one will know it is there."

Suddenly a huge Triceratops came out of the trees.

"What are you doing with my egg?"
she roared. "That egg belongs to me."

"That is *my* egg,"
Diplodocus cried,
swishing her tail.
"No it is *not*!" Triceratops
snapped.
"That egg belongs to me!"

While the two angry dinosaurs argued
and fought, the egg rolled off down
the hill into a cave.

Deep inside in the
dark and the gloom,
a sleepy Stegosaurus
was waking up
from a nap.

"Goodness me,"
she said, seeing
the egg at her toes.
"I've laid a beautiful
big, white egg."

Stegosaurus ran into the
forest and found the two
angry dinosaurs still arguing.
"I've laid an egg," she
told them.
"A big white egg?" they
both cried together.
"But that big white egg is mine."

The three dinosaurs raced back to the
cave but when they looked inside they saw ...

that the big white egg had HATCHED.

Then Triceratops saw footprints in the sand.

So Diplodocus, Triceratops and Stegosaurus
followed the footprints as fast as they could

and soon they came to the river.

They saw lots of dinosaurs

but not one was a baby just out of an egg.

They followed the footprints down to the sea ...

and there they found the
baby playing in the sand.
And that's not all …

They found his *Mom* as well ...
TYRANNOSAURUS REX—the fiercest of them all!

TYRANNOSAURUS REX
(ty-ran-oh-SAW-rus rex)

ANKYLOSAURUS
(an-KY-loh-SAW-rus)

PTERANODON
(ter-AN-o-don)

ELASMOSAURUS
(ee-laz-mo-SAW-rus)

ANATOSAURUS
(a-nat-o-SAW-rus)